Little Red Riding Hood

ILLUSTRATED BY DAVID LONG

Story adapted by
Christine Deverell

A very long time ago, so many wild beasts prowled about in the forests that no one was ever surprised to meet a wolf or a bear. A little girl, whom everyone called Red Riding Hood, lived in a cottage on the edge of a woods with her mother and father, who worked as a woodcutter. Red Riding Hood was not her real name, but it was given her because she always wore a red hooded coat that her grandmother had made for her.

Now this grandmother lived alone in a rose covered cottage on the other side of the woods, and Red Riding Hood loved to visit her. One day the little girl's mother called her and said, "Why don't you go to your grandmother's house for tea today? She has not been well, so I have baked her a

cake and made her some lemonade." Handing her the gifts in a basket, she added, "Do not stray from the path and do not stop to talk to anyone on the way."

Red Riding Hood promised to go straight to the cottage, so her mother tied on her red hood, kissed her goodbye, and off she went. She had not gone very far along

the path when she

met a wolf. "Good morning, Little Red Riding Hood, where

9

are you going today?" he asked her. "Good morning, Mr Wolf" she said, politely, "I am going to visit my grandmother." "And what are you carrying in the basket?" asked the wolf. "Cake and lemonade for our tea," Little Red Riding Hood replied.

"So where does your grandmother live?" asked the wolf in his sweetest voice. "I continue along this path, take the left path when it divides in two, and walk for another ten minutes. It's the cottage that is covered with roses." "Aha, your grandmother likes flowers, does she? Why don't you pick some of these from beside the path and take them to her?" suggested the wolf.

Then the wolf trotted off, and Little Red Riding Hood

thought it would be a
great idea to gather
a bouquet for her
grandmother. First, she
picked a few flowers from beside
the path, but then she saw
that there were some
prettier ones
under the
trees. So
she disobeyed
her mother's command, and stepped off the path.

The sun was shining through the branches and birds

were singing happily. Little Red Riding Hood suddenly remembered that she should have kept to the path and gone straight to her grandmother's cottage, so she picked up her basket and the bunch of flowers, and set off once again.

Meanwhile, the wolf had raced ahead, following Little Red Riding Hood's directions to the cottage.

"The rose covered cottage, she said, so this must be it.

Aha!" he said to himself, "Now I shall
gobble up the old grandmother, and I'll
have Little Red Riding Hood for dessert."
He knocked on the door very gently. "Lift
the latch and come in," said the old lady.
The wolf lifted the latch and burst through

the door, and gobbled

up the poor old grandmother in
one mouthful. Then he found
one of her big frilly nightcaps in
a drawer, pulled it over his ears
and jumped into bed, taking care
to draw the sheet well up under his

chin. A few moments later Red Riding Hood tapped on the
door of the cottage.

"Lift the latch and come in," said the wolf in his softest voice. But this voice did not sound like Little Red Riding Hood's grandmother, and the little girl wondered what was wrong. "Mother has sent some cake and lemonade for our tea, but grandmother, how strange your voice sounds, and why are you in bed?"

"I have a cold on my chest," answered the wolf. "Come here, my dear and sit next to me on the bed." As Red Riding Hood approached the bed, she could not believe what she saw.

"Oh, Grandmother, what big eyes you have!" she said.

"All the better to see you with, my dear," answered the wicked wolf.

"But Grandmother, what big ears you have!"

"All the better to hear you with, my dear."

"But Grandmother, what big teeth you have!"

"All the better to gobble you up with, my dear," said the wolf as he leaped out of the bed.

Little Red Riding Hood turned and ran screaming towards the door.

The wolf had just caught her red cloak

in his mouth when the door burst open, and Little Red Riding Hood's own father came rushing in.

With one blow of his axe he struck the wicked wolf

dead, and picked up poor frightened Little Red Riding Hood

in his arms and hugged her tightly.

"Oh, Father, I think the wolf must have eaten up dear Grandmother!" sobbed Little Red Riding Hood.

So he took out his knife and very carefully cut the wolf's stomach open. Inside, they found the old Grandmother safe and sound, if rather shocked, for the wolf in his greed had swallowed her whole, and his teeth had not even touched her.

They all sat down to enjoy their cake and lemonade, and Little Red Riding Hood promised her father that she would never again talk to any stranger that she might meet in the woods, and that she would always obey her mother and never stray from the path.

21